Contents

First published 2013 by Brown Watson
The Old Mill, 76 Fleckney Road
Kibworth Beauchamp
Leicestershire LE8 0HG

ISBN: 978-0-7097-2137-6
© 2013 Brown Watson, England
Printed in Malaysia

5 Minute Stories for Girls

Brown Watson
ENGLAND LE8 0HG

A Kind Heart

Princess Helena lived in a beautiful palace with wonderful gardens. Each morning, she jumped out of bed, threw open her curtains, and looked outside to see if the sun was shining.

"It's a sunny day!" she announced to her lady-in-waiting, Millie. "I'm going to play outside!" Princess Helena had her breakfast and then ran out into the garden. She skipped and twirled, and played with her dog, Buttons. Millie stayed close by, picking flowers to put in Princess Helena's bedroom.

The Princess loved to throw a
stick for Buttons to chase. She laughed
when he caught it in his mouth and
bounded back to her, yapping until she
threw the stick again.

"Oops!" she cried, as one time
she threw the stick and it landed in a
fountain. "Wait, Buttons! Don't go
in the water. I will get it for you."

As Princess Helena moved closer to the fountain, she noticed a raggedy little boy trying to hide behind it. "Hello!" she exclaimed. "Who are you?"

The little boy said nothing, but ran away. Princess Helena tried to follow him, but he ran too fast. She wondered whether he worked in the palace, and what he was doing by the fountain. She asked Millie if she knew who he was, but Millie hadn't seen him.

"If I was you, Miss, I'd stay away. He might be a thief, or a beggar!"

Each day after that, Princess Helena would play outside and try to sneak off without Millie following her. She wanted to see the boy again, and find out who he was.

Several times, she saw the boy hiding behind the fountain or peeping from behind a tree. He didn't look like trouble. In fact, he just looked hungry and frightened.

One day, while Millie was
arranging her flowers in a vase,
Princess Helena scurried off to
see if the boy was anywhere to
be found. She smiled when she
saw him, and offered him
an apple.

"I'm not going to tell anyone
you're here," she whispered.
The boy looked around
nervously. "I just want someone
to talk to. Would you like
some food?"

The boy scampered closer
and took the apple. He smiled,
but then ran away.

After that, Princess Helena made sure
she took snacks and sweets into the garden,
hoping to meet the boy again. He appeared
every day, and told the Princess his story.
He said he had no parents, but that he
loved to come to the palace to see all the
fine people in their fancy clothes.

"I don't want them to see me, though,"
he explained. "They would probably chase
me away and let the dogs come after me.
They might even call the police."

"I wouldn't let them do that!" said Princess
Helena. "I'm going to introduce you to my
mother and father. They might be royal,
but they are very kind. I will ask them if
you can live and work here, and
be my friend."

Princess Helena reached out and took the boy's
hand to lead him indoors. With a flash and a whoosh,
the boy disappeared!

Princess Helena blinked and rubbed her eyes.
The boy had gone, but in his place stood a handsome prince!
"You are so kind," he said, bowing to her. "A wicked witch
turned me into a beggar boy, and the only way to break the
spell was to find someone kind enough to trust in me. As
soon as you touched my hand, the curse was lifted. Now
we can be friends without having to hide from anyone!"

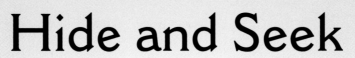

Hide and Seek

Not all princesses live in magnificent palaces. Some of them are so small you can hardly see them, and you almost never find them unless you know where to look. These are the princesses of the fairy kingdom, and they are very special indeed.

Princess Cordelia was a fairy princess, who lived in a clearing in a forest. Her home was a toadstool, where she giggled and played with her fairy friends. Their laughter was like the tinkling of tiny bells, and their gossamer wings fluttered furiously to lift them into the air and carry them through the trees and flowers.

The fairies loved to play with the forest creatures. They played chase with the birds, darting in and out of the branches of the trees. They flew over the deer that grazed on the grass, and rode on the deer's backs when their wings grew tired.

Princess Cordelia's favourite game was hide and seek. She knew some excellent places to hide from her friends. Her best spot was tucked away beneath the web of her spider friend, Mrs Spinnikins.

As Princess Cordelia flitted between
flowers, searching for her friends, she
noticed something moving. It certainly
wasn't a fairy.

"Well, look at you!" she exclaimed.
"Aren't you just the cutest, wiggliest
thing I've ever seen!"

She was talking to a plump, hairy
caterpillar that was nestling on a leaf.
It didn't reply, but just waved its
head around and smiled.

Princess Cordelia stopped playing hide
and seek and shouted to her friends.
"Come and look what I have found!"

Very gently, Princess Cordelia plucked the leaf from its stem, and carried it back to her toadstool home. Her friends flew with her, giggling as the caterpillar wiggled and jiggled.

"Mummy!" called Princess Cordelia, as she flew down to their house. "Please can I keep this caterpillar as a pet? I promise I will look after it, and feed it every day. I can collect all of its favourite leaves, and bring it raindrops to drink. I will keep it safe from any birds that try to peck at it."

Cordelia's mother thought that the caterpillar was adorable, and agreed that Cordelia could keep it nearby. "But you must promise to take good care of it," she said, "and not get bored of looking after it.

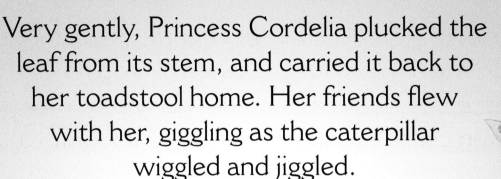
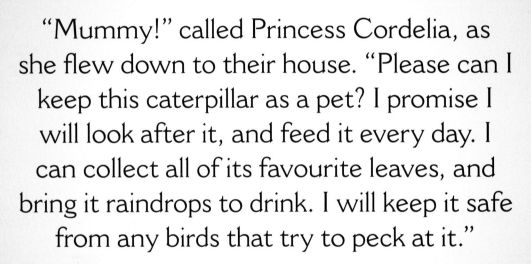

And if it ever wants to go back to its own home, then you must accept that."

Princess Cordelia hugged her mother, and then found a safe place for the caterpillar on its leaf. Each day, she checked that her pet was happy. Her friends often called round with fresh plants for it to eat.

One morning, Princess Cordelia picked up the leaf and showed it to her mother. The caterpillar looked different, and she was worried. "It isn't wiggling as much as normal," she said, "and its skin looks a funny colour."

Her mother agreed, but told Cordelia to put the leaf back into the shade and then come inside to tidy her room. "You can check on it again soon," she promised.

The fairy princess did as she was told. She tidied her room faster than ever before, and then hurried back outside to her pet. It had disappeared!

Cordelia searched everywhere, but the caterpillar was nowhere to be seen. She burst into tears.

For days and days, Princess Cordelia looked for her little wiggly friend. She brought fresh food and water, and sat and watched for any tiny movement that might be the caterpillar.

One day, a colourful butterfly fluttered towards her. It hovered by her side, and then smiled and wiggled its head. "It's you!" cried Princess Cordelia. "Of course! Caterpillars turn into butterflies. That's why you were hiding!"

Stars of the Show

Sophie and Becky are best friends. They go to different schools, but see each other every week when it is time for ballet class. Today, the sun is shining, the birds are singing, and the girls are skipping along happily in front of Becky's mum. They are very excited. Today is the day that their teacher, Miss Franklin, is going to tell them about the end of term show.

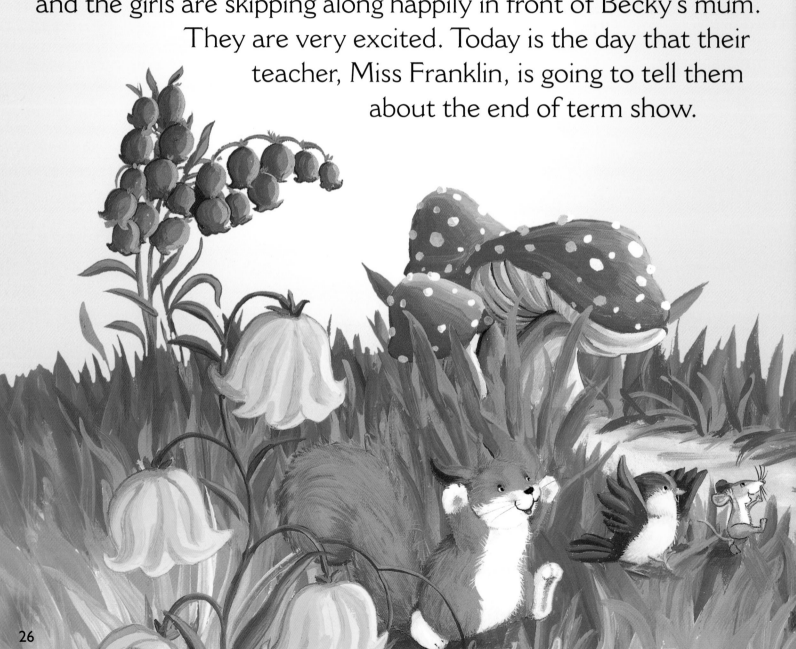

Becky wants to be a princess, but she hasn't been dancing for very long. She knows she will only get a small role. "Hello, Mrs Bunny!" she whispers to the rabbit hopping in the grass nearby. "Please let Sophie and me get good parts in the show!"

Sophie gazes at the animals and plants around her. "I wish I could be a flower," she sighs.

The class starts, and nothing is said about the show. The girls know that they must not talk during practice, so they are very good and stay quiet. They are so excited, they can hardly keep their arms straight and their toes pointed!

When they take a break, the girls sit next to Tom. He is older and has been in a show before. "What's it like?" they ask. "And when will Miss Franklin tell us about it?"

Tom smiles. "It's really good fun," he says. "But it's very hard work. We have to practise all the time, even at home. Miss Franklin won't say anything about it until the end of the lesson."

That seems like ages away!

Sophie tries to concentrate on her dancing, but she can't stop thinking about the show. Becky laughs as she watches from the back of the class. "Sophie," she says, "you're really good at ballet, but you keep forgetting your steps!"

Sophie tries to concentrate. She pretends that she is a flower, blooming and swaying in the sunshine. Miss Franklin is impressed. "Well done, Sophie!" she says, "Now then, everyone, gather round. I have some exciting news for you all."

The dancers sit cross-legged in front of their teacher. One by one, they are told what parts they are going to dance. Sophie and Becky hold hands and wait for their names to be called.

First, Miss Franklin starts with the new dancers. Sophie is chosen to be a bluebell! Maybe wishes do come true after all? She keeps her fingers crossed that Becky gets a good part.

More names are read out, and still Becky has not been called. Then Miss Franklin says they need a fluffy rabbit, and she thinks Becky will be perfect. Becky gasps. She is excited, but a little bit nervous as well.

As the dancers meet their parents to head home, the girls hug each other and giggle. They tell their great news to Becky's mum, who promises to help them practise as much as they can.

Tom was right. It is hard work, with lots and lots of practising, but it's really good fun. They giggle when they try on their costumes. Sophie loves her bluebell hat, but Jake can't see a thing in his bird costume. Becky hops about in front of him while he crawls around, trying to find the best way to see out of his mask.

It seems like no time until
it is the night of the show.
Backstage, everyone is
excited. They peep round the
curtains to find their families
sitting in the audience.
"I can see my dad!"
cries Jake.

"Well, at least you can see
something!" laughs Becky.

As the music begins, they
dance onto the stage
and try to remember
all of their steps.
Jake lifts up his
beak so that he can
see what he is doing.

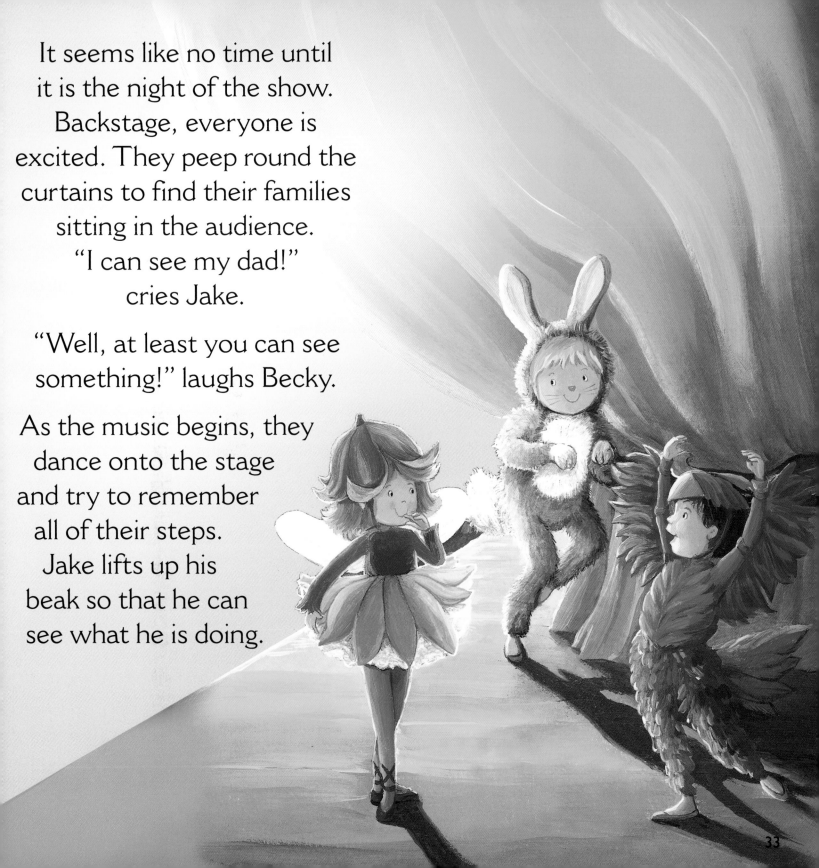

The whole group dances their very best. The main woodland characters have the trickiest moves, and Becky feels very proud that she keeps up with them. She can see her mum watching and clapping, and it makes her feel glowing and warm inside.

When the flowers perform their solo dance, the crowd cheers loudly. Sophie concentrates hard and remembers all of her steps.

It seems like it's only five minutes before all the dances are finished, and the ballet school lines up across the stage. They curtsey and bow to the audience, who stand up to give them a big round of applause. Someone even whistles and whoops!

"I love being a Bunny," smiles Becky, "and you really suit being a bluebell, Sophie!" They hold hands and laugh as Jake bows again and his mask slips back onto his face.

Flight of Fancy

Princess Julia was a very lucky girl. She knew that she was, and usually she was very grateful. She had a beautiful home, with fine food and friendly servants, and a mother and father who loved her very much.

Sometimes, though, it felt like a hard job to do. She had to be on her best behaviour all the time, and sit with grown-ups who talked about things she didn't understand. Her gorgeous dresses were heavy and tight, and meant that she couldn't play outside.

Worse than any of that, though, was the fact that she had no brothers or sisters to keep her company. She often got lost in a fantasy world filled with unicorns and fairies to stop her from feeling lonely.

Princess Julia's mother often watched her daughter and saw her drift off into a faraway dream world. When that happened, she tried to excuse Julia and let her leave the room. Julia would hug her mother and then scamper off.

When she was on her own, Princess Julia gathered her colouring pens and paper, and let herself get lost in her dreams. She drew the places from her imagination, and filled them with magical creatures.

As Julia put on her best blue dress for another royal banquet, her mother entered the room. "I have some good news," she said, popping Julia's crown on her head. "There will be a girl of your age at the table today! Her name is Emily and she is the Emperor's daughter."

The two girls made friends immediately, and after their meal they were allowed to leave the table. Princess Julia took Emily to her room, and showed her all of her drawings.

Emily gasped when she saw how many wonderful lands Julia had dreamed of. "They're amazing!" she smiled, clapping her hands with delight.

"Really?" asked Princess Julia. "You don't think they're silly? I keep them secret in case people laugh at my daydream places."

"Not at all," assured Emily. "In fact, I have an even bigger secret to share with you. Do you promise not to tell?"

The two girls huddled together and Emily opened her purse. She took out a sparkling emerald ring and placed it on her finger. She squeezed Julia's hand and told her not to let go, and then blew on the jewel and closed her eyes. Julia scrunched her eyes shut too.

The girls clung to each other, and Princess Julia felt a warm wind rushing through her hair.
It felt like they were flying! They bumped down on the ground and opened their eyes.

"Where are we?" whispered Julia.

Emily let go of her hand and pointed up a hill. "Look around," she said. "It is exactly as you imagined it."

Sure enough, as Princess Julia gazed around her, she began to recognise the places she had drawn. She jumped to her feet and started to run. "This is amazing!" she cried. A cluster of fairies gathered around and beckoned to her with their tiny hands.

Emily and Julia ran and laughed and played with the fairies. They rode on a unicorn and flew high above the treetops. Emily explained that the magic lasted for an hour, and then they would be whisked back to their own lives.

"But time in our world will stay the same, so no one will know we are missing," she said. "And the next time I see you, we can use the ring again!"

Princess Julia smiled, and promised herself that she would draw even more exciting pictures before Emily and her father's next visit. Being a princess had just got even better!

Dreams Come True

Abbie loved ponies. She dreamed of owning a pony of her own, and riding it every day. Sadly, though, Abbie's family was very poor. They could never afford a pony. They all lived and worked at the royal palace, and only earned enough for food and a few simple clothes.

Abbie worked with her mother and sisters. While their mother cooked, the girls did all the other jobs that needed doing. They peeled the vegetables and scrubbed the dishes. They washed the royal clothes, and kept the kitchen clean and tidy.

It was hard work, but Abbie didn't mind.
At least she was with her family every day.
She laughed and joked with her sisters while
they hung out washing, or helped each
other put away the pots and pans.

Abbie's father was the royal groom. Whenever she could, Abbie would finish her work in the kitchen and run to the stables to help her father.

Her father was grateful, and Abbie loved working with the ponies. She would happily stay until after dark, sweeping and scrubbing and putting things away. She didn't even mind mucking out.

As a reward, Abbie's father would give her a handful of horse treats, and she would stand in the meadows and feed the ponies.

One day, as Abbie cleared dirty straw in the stables, she heard a voice. It was the Prince! She hid in an empty stall so that she wouldn't be in the way.

"Oh, Captain!" she heard the Prince sigh. "Being a prince is so lonely! People would think I am crazy if they heard me speaking to you, but I have no one else to talk to!"

Abbie tried to stay hidden, but a piece of straw tickled her nose and made her sneeze. The Prince looked around, and saw Abbie sheltering behind a wall. He seemed surprised at first, but then he smiled.

The Prince held out his hand. "Don't be shy," he said. "I don't mind you being here. Come and say hello to Captain."

Abbie moved close enough to stroke the beautiful horse's muzzle. He made a gentle nickering noise and pushed his nose into her hand.

"Would you like to ride him?" offered the Prince. He helped Abbie climb up onto Captain's back. She couldn't stop smiling as she trotted around. But then an almighty bang made Captain bolt, and he sped off at full speed. Poor Abbie clung on for dear life.

Captain ran and ran. The Prince tried to follow, but he was soon left far behind. Thankfully, as they reached the edge of the forest, Captain began to slow down. He picked his way carefully along a woodland path until they reached a clearing in the trees.

Before Abbie could climb down, she heard a rustling noise. A ghostly white shape was coming towards them from the gloom of the branches.

Abbie held her breath as a magnificent unicorn stepped into the clearing. It looked directly at Abbie and Captain, and then Abbie heard a magical voice. It seemed to be right inside her head.

"Welcome to the enchanted forest," said the unicorn. "I am here to make your wishes come true! Think of three things that your heart desires, and they shall be yours."

It was easy for Abbie to think of three things. She wished that her family didn't have to work so hard for so little money. She wished that the Prince would be happy, and not lonely any more. Her one wish just for herself was to have a pony of her own.

"Your wishes shall come true!" thought the unicorn, and the words tinkled inside Abbie's head. "Go home now, kind girl, and tell your loved ones what has happened."

Captain gently carried Abbie back to the royal stables. Her family ran to her. "We were so worried about you!" they said. Abbie told them all about the unicorn and her wishes, and they hugged her tightly.

True to its word, the unicorn made Abbie's dreams come true. Her family no longer struggled for money, and the Prince fell in love with Abbie and asked her to marry him. When Abbie agreed, he gave her the best engagement present ever – a pony called Diamond, of course!

Come Out to Play!

Once upon a time, not that long ago, four princesses lived together in a beautiful palace. The sisters had more toys than they could play with, and more dresses than they could possibly wear.

One of these princesses was called Maricel, and she loved her fine clothes more than anything. Every day, she would choose a new outfit, and try it on in front of the mirror. She gazed at her reflection, and said a silent thank you for how lucky she was. Maricel's three sisters loved their dresses, too, but they didn't wear them every day. They preferred to wear ordinary clothes so that they could play outside in the garden. The palace grounds were enormous, and full of trees to climb and hiding spots to play hide and seek.

Princess Maricel watched them jumping around and getting dirty. She wasn't sure that a proper princess should climb trees or run around in the garden.

Each morning, as Princess Maricel put on her fine clothes, her sisters would beg her to join in their games.

"Come and play outside!" they shrieked and laughed. "It's so much more fun than staying indoors! Look – there are butterflies to chase, and flowers to collect, if you don't want to get messy."

Maricel sometimes wondered about playing out, but she worried that her fine dresses would be ruined. Instead, she got out her dolls and dressed them up in lots of wonderful outfits. Her sisters stopped asking if she wanted to join them outside.

Princess Maricel's mother worried about her,
and spoke to her one day.

"A King and Queen are visiting soon, and bringing
their daughter with them. Maybe she will join in
your games and play with your toys?"

Maricel was very excited, and couldn't wait to have a
new friend. When they arrived, she was overjoyed to
see that the new princess wore fine clothes with lace
and gold trimmings that glittered and sparkled.

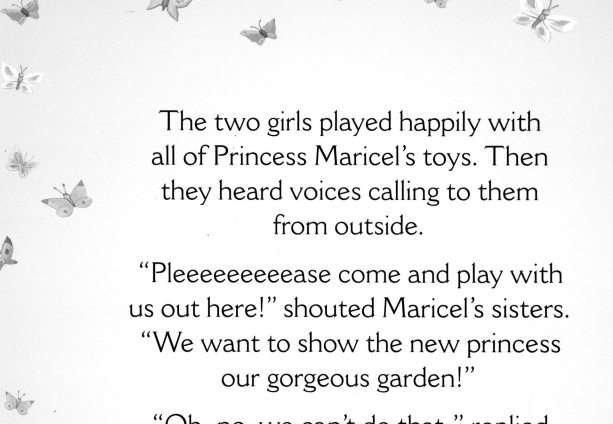

The two girls played happily with all of Princess Maricel's toys. Then they heard voices calling to them from outside.

"Pleeeeeeeeease come and play with us out here!" shouted Maricel's sisters. "We want to show the new princess our gorgeous garden!"

"Oh, no, we can't do that," replied Maricel. "Our dresses are too fancy! Look at you, you're all dirty and have leaves in your hair! We're happy playing indoors with all of the toys."

"Why don't we go outside and play?" asked the new princess. "Your garden looks amazing, and your sisters are having so much fun! Listen, I can hear them laughing and screaming."

"But that isn't how a princess should behave!" said Princess Maricel.

"Why ever not?" asked her new friend. "Surely the best thing about being a princess is that you can do whatever you want! I do love your toys, and I am having fun, but I want to play outside as well. Come on!"

The new princess gave Maricel a hug, and then ran out of the room. Soon, Princess Maricel could hear an extra voice outside. "Race you to the fountain!"

She picked up her doll and then put it down again. It did sound like fun out there – and she was missing it.

Before she could change her mind, Princess Maricel ran to her wardrobe and hunted around for a new outfit. This time she wasn't looking for a fancy dress, with sparkling jewels. She needed something to play out in!

In no time at all, Maricel had joined her sisters and their new friend in the garden. She laughed and skipped, and even lay down on the grass and rolled down the sloping lawns. She landed in a heap at the bottom, on top of her sisters, then jumped up and grabbed a ball. "Who wants to play?" she called, and they all ran after her.

She wished she had done this a long time ago. It really was fun. That's what being a princess should be like!

Swan Sisters

Princess Clara was a happy princess. She was happiest of all when the sun was shining and she could leave the palace behind and run outdoors.

She loved to feel the sun on her face, the breeze in her hair, and the grass brushing against her ankles.

The only thing that made Clara sad was thinking about her lost sister. Clara's parents once had two daughters. When Clara was a tiny baby, a wicked wizard had cast a spell on Clara's big sister, and she had never been seen again. Her parents would not allow anyone to talk about their oldest child.

Sometimes, Princess Clara would chase the dragonflies around the royal lake, and pretend they were fairies. She would talk and sing to them, and without her parents to watch over her, she would daydream about her big sister.

"Fairies, fairies, you must know, where did my lovely sister go?" she sang, as she raced up and down.

Of course, the dragonflies were only insects, and couldn't talk. They skittered around on their gossamer wings, and Clara chased them until she was tired.

One day, as Princess Clara lay on
her tummy in the grass, she heard
an unusual tinkling noise.

"Was that you?" she smiled at a bee flying past.
But she heard the noise again, and it definitely
wasn't a buzzing. She looked quizzically
at a ladybird on a nearby flower.
"Was that YOU?" she asked.

"No, silly, it was me!" tinkled a tiny, bell-like
voice. Princess Clara gasped. There, in front
of her very eyes, was a tiny fairy! She was
dressed in pink, with wings that beat so fast
they were a blur, and a huge wand nearly
as big as the fairy was.

Princess Clara rubbed her eyes and then listened as the fairy spoke to her. She explained that she had a special surprise for Clara, but that she must do exactly as the fairy said.

The fairy told Clara to go down to the lake and look for the very smallest swan that swam there.

"You will need to row across the lake – you will be careful, won't you?" fluttered the fairy.

"Of course I will," answered Clara. "But what do I do when I find the smallest swan?"

The fairy finished her instructions. Clara must carefully gather up the swan and row with it back to shore. Then she should carry the swan back to the palace, and run a lovely bath for it to swim in.

"But wh–?" Clara started to ask, and the fairy pressed her wand against Clara's lips. She waved it in the direction of the lake, and Clara got to her feet and ran off to find her boat.

As Princess Clara stood in her room, waiting for the bathtub to fill up, she looked at the swan that she had brought from the lake. The swan looked back at her and blinked, and then hopped straight up and into the water.

With a flash and a bang, the swan disappeared. Clara squealed, as there in its place was a girl. She looked a lot like Clara, but with beautiful dark hair and a dress made of swan feathers.

The girl hugged Clara, and tears began to roll down her cheeks. "Clara," she said, "I am your long lost sister! You have broken the sorcerer's spell, and now I can live as a princess once more!"

The girls held each other tightly, and then ran through the palace to find the King and Queen. Imagine how happy they were to see both of their daughters together!

Wishes Come True

This is Belinda. You might be wondering why a princess is digging in the garden. But Belinda isn't a real princess. She pretends that she is, and dresses up in her crown no matter what jobs she is doing.

Belinda knows what it is like to be a princess, as she works at the palace and sees real princesses all the time. They parade around in their fine clothes, and look down their nose at the people they see working. "If I was a real princess, I'd be as kind as I could," thought Belinda.

Belinda loves working in the garden. She knows the name of every flower that grows there, and what kind of insects like each one. Imagine her surprise when she sees something that she has never seen before! It is a cluster of spotty red toadstools.

"I'm sure these weren't here yesterday," says Belinda. "I wonder if they're poisonous?"

When Belinda stands up to go and ask the gardener about the toadstools, she notices something unusual. "These toadstools make a perfect circle!" she exclaims. "They could be a fairy ring!"

Nervously, Belinda puts one foot inside the circle. She feels a tingling in her toes, and little sparks jump up her leg. She takes a deep breath and steps right inside the ring.

Each of the toadstools begins to shimmer, and stars explode all around Belinda's ears. Her whole body trembles and she can hear a beautiful, musical humming noise.

In a flash, a host of fairies flutter towards Belinda. They are so pretty, and Belinda can't help smiling. It's like a shower of happiness has just washed over her! A tiny fairy in a pink dress whispers in Belinda's ear.

"We can grant one wish for you – what will it be?"

Belinda thinks for a moment, and then decides. "I'd like to be a real princess for a while!" she says.

The fairies all join hands, and Belinda closes her eyes and crosses her fingers.

The tingling grows stronger, and more stars flash all around. Belinda looks down and sees that her ragged gardening dress has been transformed into a beautiful gown, with frills and ruffles. She puts a hand up to her head, and finds that her crown has gone, and has been replaced with a real diamond tiara.

"Ooooh!" she squeals. "Am I really a princess? How exciting! Now then, what shall I do first?"

She thinks hard and then decides she is going to share her good luck. Quietly, she tiptoes towards the palace. As she goes past the gardens, she finds lots of golden coins in her pocket. She has an idea!

Belinda scatters the coins amongst the flowers and on the lawn. Then she runs into the palace and starts to explore. It is truly amazing! The chairs are made of gold, and decorated with jewels. The tables are laid with fine foods, and there are enormous bowls of fruit and sweets in every room.

Belinda carries on exploring, and tiptoes up the stairs to the bedrooms. She finds a room fit for a princess, and lies down on the bed. It is so soft and squishy! It is tempting to fall asleep, but she is too excited. She doesn't want to waste the precious time she has being a princess.

Instead, she peeps out of the window to see what is happening in the gardens.

With a big smile on her face, Belinda goes back outside. From her magic fairy ring, she can see lots of people, shouting and exclaiming as they find the gold coins.

The King is quite puzzled, but he joins in the hunt. "There's one!" he bellows, showing the maid where to find a coin. "Finders keepers, eh, Mrs Crumb?" Mrs Crumb says thank you, and puts the coin in her pocket.

Belinda watches happily as they gather more coins. "I said I'd be a kind princess, and I have kept my word!" she thinks to herself, smiling.

The Dancing Princess

Princess Larina loved to dance. She had lessons every day, and never got tired of dancing. Her teacher said she moved beautifully, and so did her parents.

"Oh, but you're only saying that because you're my parents!" she said, modestly.

Her father protested, and promised to arrange a dancing competition for everyone in the land.

"People will come from far away to show off their talents," he said. "Then you will find out if you really are a great dancer!"

The Princess was very excited, and whirled round and round with her dance teacher.

The King made sure that word spread about the dancing competition. It was to be held at the palace, and anyone younger than sixteen was allowed to enter.

Princess Larina practised every day. She was feeling quite nervous. She didn't want to win just because she was the King's daughter, and she was scared that she might not be as good as her teacher said.

On the day of the contest, she woke up very early. There was a lot of chatter and noise coming from outside, so she looked out of her window. Crowds of people had gathered at the palace to try to win the prize. Now Larina was very scared!

As Larina put on her dance costume, and wondered if she would be able to eat any breakfast, she heard someone call her name.

She looked around her, but no one was there. Then, outside the window, she saw something very strange indeed. It was a young boy, peeping into her room.
How had he got there?

Princess Larina walked to the window to say hello. "Who are you, and how are you – oh!" she exclaimed. The boy was sitting on a flying carpet, hovering high in the air!

The Princess couldn't believe
her eyes – or her ears.

"My name is Prince Param," said the
boy. "I heard about your dance contest,
and I have come to win it," he smiled.
"For I am the finest dancer for
thousands of miles!"

Princess Larina tilted her head to one
side and looked at the boy. He did look
quite royal, and he was on a flying
carpet. But was he telling the truth
about his dancing?

"Well," she said. "We shall see about
that!" She put on her dancing shoes
and twirled out of her room.

The dance competition was tough.
There were so many good dancers,
all trying their very best. The judges
decided to make it an instant knockout.
The dancers swayed and swirled until
a judge tapped them and told them to sit
down, one by one. Prince Param was
as good as he had said. He moved so
gracefully it was magical to watch him.
Soon, it was just the Prince and
Princess on the dance floor.

The Prince took Larina's hand
and together they leaped and span.
Larina began to wonder if she could
dance any longer. She had actually
danced for so long that even she was
beginning to feel tired!

Finally, the Prince stood back and
watched Larina dance alone. The judges
all clapped as it became clear that the
Princess was the winner.

"You truly are the champion,"
announced Prince Param.
"For I have a confession to make.
My magic shoes helped me, but you
dance without magic. Your dancing is
amazing, and now the whole
country knows it!"

Teething Problems

Flossie is a little fairy with a very special job to do.
She is going to learn how to be a tooth fairy!
Her big sister, Faye, takes Flossie along for her
first day at school.

Flossie's teacher is Princess Elvine. She used to be a tooth fairy,
but now she is in charge of training all the new recruits.
She stays in Fairyland and makes sure all of the young fairies
return home safely.

"Good morning, Flossie," says Princess Elvine.
"I see you have a shiny new satchel, the colour of
buttercups. It's lovely!"

"Thank you, Miss," says Flossie, who is a little bit shy.
Then Princess Elvine hands her a sparkling wand, and
Flossie forgets to be nervous. It glistens and glimmers
like thousands of fireflies all shining at once!

The trainee tooth fairies have lots to learn. Every day, there is a new lesson. They practise their secret skills over and over again.

A good tooth fairy must be able to fly silently, even when she is carrying a heavy bag full of coins and teeth. At first, Flossie's shiny yellow satchel sounds like the whole percussion section of an orchestra: CRASH! CLATTER! TING! CHING!

All the fairies learn how to zoom down to earth on shiny moonbeams. Sliding down isn't so hard, but stopping at the bottom is the tricky part!
"WHEEEEEEEE!" laughs Flossie.
"Shhhh!" giggles her friend Patsy.

There are spells to help them find the right children, and spells to let the fairies fly into bedrooms even if the windows are closed.

Princess Elvine shows the fairies how to use their wands and say the right spell to whisk out the teeth from underneath a pillow.

One morning, as Princess Elvine takes the register, she makes a grand announcement. "School will finish late tonight," she says, "as you will all be making your first outing to collect teeth. I hope you are all ready for the challenge!"

Flossie and Patsy look at each other nervously.
They are very excited, but scared too!

As night falls, the fairies form pairs and check
they have everything they need.
Wand…coins…list of teeth to collect…
and very importantly, tooth bags
to carry their precious finds.

Flossie and Patsy say their spells to find their first home and fly inside a little girl's bedroom. They can barely contain their excitement as they gaze down on the girl, sleeping peacefully. Patsy wiggles her wand and says her spell to sneak the tooth out from under the pillow. But nothing appears.

"Try again!" whispers Flossie, super quietly. Patsy does, but still there is no tooth.

"You try!" says Patsy, so Flossie waves her wand. The fairies are starting to worry. Patsy even flies bravely up to the girl and feels under her pillow. She is so close that the girl nearly blows her away when she breathes out!

Flossie is extremely nervous
and nearly jumps out of her wings
when a fat, friendly mouse squeaks
at her. "Are you looking
for a tooth?" he asks.
"This one was on the floor
when I arrived earlier."

Flossie and Patsy are so relieved! "Oh, thank you Mr Mouse! Now we can carry on with the rest of our work for tonight!" They give him one of their coins, and then fly off to visit a little boy who is dreaming about a unicorn. Thankfully, his tooth is exactly where it should be, and all of their magic works perfectly.

As the sun begins to rise in the morning sky, the fairies hitch a ride back up to Fairyland.

Flossie and Patsy tell Princess Elvine all about their adventure. She is glad that it all worked out in the end. Flossie can't wait to tell her sister about it, too, but before she has finished her tale, she is fast asleep. It has been a very hard night, after all!

The Magic Shoes

Princess Rosie is a very good girl. Every morning, she does her lessons. She has a tutor, who teaches her maths and spellings. She often sits with her mother, too, and they practise her lessons together.

Today, she has spent a long time learning her times tables. The queen is very pleased with her. "I think you have worked really hard today," she smiles, and kisses her daughter. "Now you can go out and play. Don't forget to come back in time for your dancing lesson!"

Princess Rosie would never forget her dancing lesson. It's her favourite! She picks up her toy doll and skips outside. She is going to collect flowers to bring home for all of her teachers.

The little princess skips through the meadows and picks some beautiful flowers. Soon, she starts to yawn, and lies down beneath a tree for a rest. Before long, she is fast asleep!

As Princess Rosie snoozes, she doesn't realise that a little pixie is watching over her. He is not a naughty sprite, but likes to spread happiness wherever he can. It's time for some magic! He mutters a few words, and then scatters a sprinkling of pixie dust over the sleepy princess.

The Princess wriggles and mumbles, and soon she is having the most fantastic dream.

She dreams that she is the best dancer in the kingdom, and never gets tired of skipping and twirling. Her doll, Stacey Starr, has come to life and is dancing with her, too!

Together, they laugh and leap through candy-coloured trees next to candyfloss lawns. Princess Rosie looks down at her feet and sees that she and Stacey Starr are both wearing magical ballet shoes. They sparkle and shimmer and make the dancers feel as light as air!

The magic shoes carry them out of the woods and into the town. Everywhere they dance, they gather more people. The villagers run out of their houses and join in the dancing. Princess Rosie links arms with her best friend Jemima, and teaches her some tricky new steps. But they don't feel tricky when she is wearing the magical shoes!

The streets are full of people laughing and pirouetting. Stacey Starr is doing a foxtrot with two friendly rabbits!

"I want to dance forever!" cries Princess Rosie, but soon her friends are too tired to keep up. Rosie waves goodbye and dances down the street with Stacey Starr by her side.

As the laughter fades, Princess Rosie begins to wake up. She blinks her eyes and stretches her arms. Then she shakes her head and rubs her face. Stacey Starr is lying still on the grass beside her.

"What happened there?" she thinks to herself. "Was it all just a dream? Oh, why did I have to stop dancing?"

The cheeky little pixie watches from a safe hiding place. He hopes he has made Princess Rosie happy, not sad.

The pixie hops from foot to foot and casts another small spell. Princess Rosie feels a tingling in her toes. When she looks at her feet, she lets out a small shriek.

"My feet! My shoes! They're just like the ones in my dream! Oh, Stacey Starr, let us run home as fast as we can and show my mother! I have magic shoes – wheeeeeee!"

The Princess scoops up her doll, and the flowers she has picked, and rushes back to the palace.

"Mummy! Mummy!" she cries. "Wait until you hear what has happened!"

The wise queen listens to her excited daughter with a smile. She has spotted the little pixie hiding nearby, so she isn't surprised at all.

"You are a very lucky girl," says the queen to Princess Rosie. "Look after them well, and you will be able to dance magically whenever you want to. And I wouldn't be surprised if Stacey Starr and all of her friends dance with you too!"

The Little Mermaid

Far, far beneath the waves there was a kingdom like none you ever saw. It was full of mermaids and mermen, with tails instead of legs. They swam and played with the fishes, and chased the dolphins near the surface.

The King had six beautiful daughters, who loved to sit on the rocks and watch the humans who sailed past. The youngest of these daughters sat there every night, and sang sweetly for the sailors to hear.

One stormy night, as she watched
a handsome prince sail past, she
heard the booming sound of
thunder and saw the waves swell
high over the sides of his boat.
The prince was thrown overboard
and disappeared into the foam as
the sea crashed and thrashed.

The littlest mermaid dived into the storm and pulled the drowning prince to the surface. She carried him to shore and laid him gently on the sandy beach. As she gazed across at him, hoping he would wake, she heard somebody approach.

The mermaid hid behind a rock and watched a pretty young girl kneel next to the prince and stroke his hair. He spluttered and coughed, and when he opened his eyes and saw the girl, he smiled.

Sadly, the mermaid swam back to her underwater world, but she could not stop thinking about the prince. Every night, she returned to the same place in the hope of seeing him. She would sit on a rock and wait until the sky grew pale, but he never returned to the beach.

The mermaid felt that her heart would break. She no longer enjoyed her life beneath the waves. All she could dream about was having legs instead of a tail, and finding her true love.

She decided to ask the evil sea witch for one of her potions.

The wicked witch lived in a dark cave, surrounded by poisonous weeds and electric eels. She cackled when she saw the little mermaid.

"I knew you were coming, my beauty! And here is the potion you desire."

The mermaid reached out her hand, but the sea witch snatched the bottle away. "It does not come for free!" she leered. She explained that the mermaid must pay with her beautiful voice, and never speak nor sing again.

"When you walk on your new legs, the pain will be greater than you can imagine," she hooted. "It will feel like a hundred knives in each foot. And be warned – if the prince marries another, you cannot return to your life as a mermaid, but will be cast into the sea as foam on the waves."

The mermaid wanted legs so badly that she accepted the witch's terms. She swam close to shore and then drank the foul-tasting liquid. A pain shot through her tail, as if someone had chopped it in two with an axe. She dragged herself to the sand and then fainted.

When she awoke, she was gazing straight into the eyes of her prince. He gently lifted her up and took her to his palace. She could not speak, but the prince spent hours each day with her and was glad of her company. They danced together, although each step with her new legs felt as if she was dancing on swords.

One day, the prince held her hand and explained that he was getting married. "I have finally found the girl who saved me from drowning, and she is happy to be my wife!" said the prince.

The little mermaid knew this wasn't really true, but she could not say a word. She sadly watched the prince prepare for his royal wedding.

That night, the mermaid heard voices calling to her from the sea. Her sisters had come to help.

"Take this magical knife and use it to kill the prince," they said. "It is the only way for you to get your tail back and come home to us. If you do not, you will be taken into the clouds to live with the air spirits."

The little mermaid took the knife, but she knew she could never hurt the prince. After her sisters had gone, she threw the weapon far out into the ocean.

A warm breeze swept
up her body, and she
lingered in the clouds,
watching over her true
love for the rest of time.